To the real Patrick, of course
K. L.

For Gran
A. J.

First published in the United States 1999
by Dial Books for Young Readers
A member of Penguin Putnam Inc.
375 Hudson Street • New York, New York 10014

Published in Great Britain 1998
by Bloomsbury Publishing Plc as *What!*
Text copyright © 1998 by Kate Lum
Pictures copyright © 1998 by Adrian Johnson
All rights reserved
Printed in Belgium by Proost N.V. on acid-free paper
First Edition
5 7 9 10 8 6 4

Library of Congress Cataloging in Publication Data
is available upon request
LC: 98-19642• ISBN 0-8037-2382-2

The artwork was prepared using acrylic paint on art board.

WHAT!
CRIED GRANNY
An *Almost* Bedtime Story

by **Kate Lum** pictures by **Adrian Johnson**

Dial Books for Young Readers ◭ New York

Once upon a time there was a boy named Patrick who was having his first sleep-over at his Granny's house.

As the sun began to set, Granny said, "Patrick, dear boy!
It will be dark soon. Time to get ready for bed."
"But, Granny," said Patrick....

"I don't **HAVE** a bed here."

"WHAT?"

cried Granny. She ran
out to her yard
where some tall
trees were growing, and
chopped one down.

She carried it to her workroom, opened her toolbox, and made Patrick a fine bed.

Then she painted it a restful shade of blue, put a comfy red mattress on it, and took it to the bedroom.

"There you are dear boy," said Granny. "Now climb into bed, lay your head on the pillow, and sail off to Dreamland!"

"But, Granny," said Patrick....

"I don't HAVE a pillow here!"

"WHAT?!?" cried Granny.
She ran out to her henhouse, woke up the chickens,
and collected a big batch of feathers.

She took them to her sewing room where she made
a bag out of cloth. Then she stuffed it with the feathers,
sewed it up neatly, and gave it to Patrick.

"There you are, dear boy," said Granny.
"Now climb into bed, lay your head on the pillow,
tuck the blanket under your chin, and I'll kiss you
good night."

"But, Granny," said Patrick....
"I don't HAVE a blanket here!"

"WHAAAT??!!??" cried Granny.
She ran outside and headed for the hills where
a flock of fat sheep were snoozing. She sheared
off some of their wool and ran right back home.

She took the wool to her basement, spun it into yarn, knitted a fuzzy warm blanket, and dyed it the prettiest shade of twilight purple. When it was dry, she carried it upstairs and spread it on the bed.

"Now, dear boy," said Granny, "climb into bed, lay your head on the pillow, tuck the blanket under your chin, give your teddy bear a hug, and turn out the light!"

"But, Granny," said Patrick....

She grabbed her emergency sewing kit, tore down the living room curtains, cut, sewed, stuffed, added button eyes and a red ribbon, and made a teddy bear for Patrick.

"NOW, PATRICK!" cried Granny.

"CLIMB into bed.

LAY your head on the pillow.

TUCK the blanket under your chin.

GIVE your teddy bear a hug.

And ...

GO TO SLEEP!"

"But, Granny," said Patrick. . . .

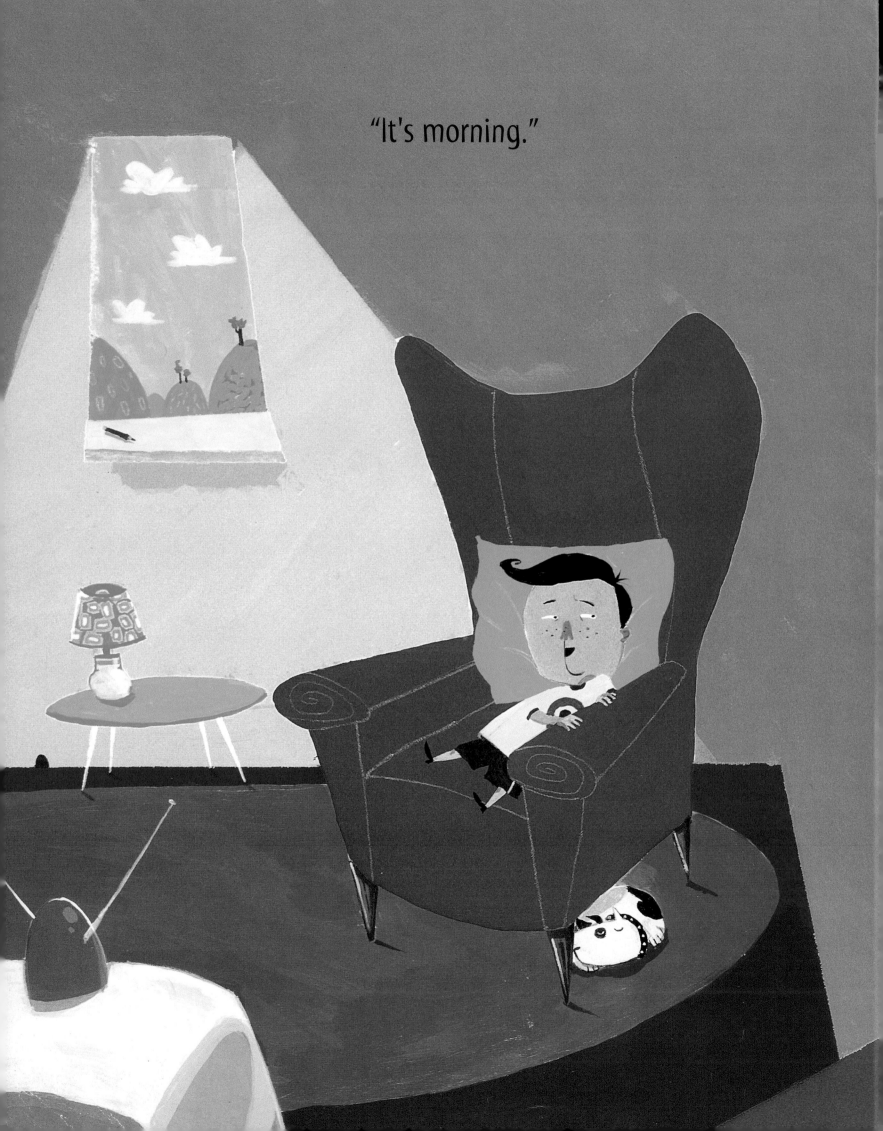

"It's morning."

"WHAAAAAAA!!!!"

cried Granny.